For my family – with whom
I've been truly blessed

Text and illustrations copyright © 2011 Rebecca Elliott
This edition copyright © 2011 Lion Hudson

The moral rights of the author
have been asserted

A Lion Children's Book
an imprint of
Lion Hudson plc
Wilkinson House, Jordan Hill Road,
Oxford OX2 8DR, England
www.lionhudson.com
Paperback ISBN 978 0 7459 6270 2
US hardback ISBN 978 0 7459 6323 5

First paperback edition 2011
1 3 5 7 9 10 8 6 4 2 0
First US hardback edition 2012
1 3 5 7 9 10 8 6 4 2 0

A catalogue record for this book is available
from the British Library

Typeset in Temble ITC
Printed in China January 2012 (manufacturer LH17)

Distributed by:
UK: Marston Book Services Ltd, PO Box 269, Abingdon, Oxon OX14 4YN
USA: Trafalgar Square Publishing, 814 N Franklin Street, Chicago, IL 60610
USA Christian Market: Kregel Publications, PO Box 2607, Grand Rapids, MI 49501

Zoo Girl

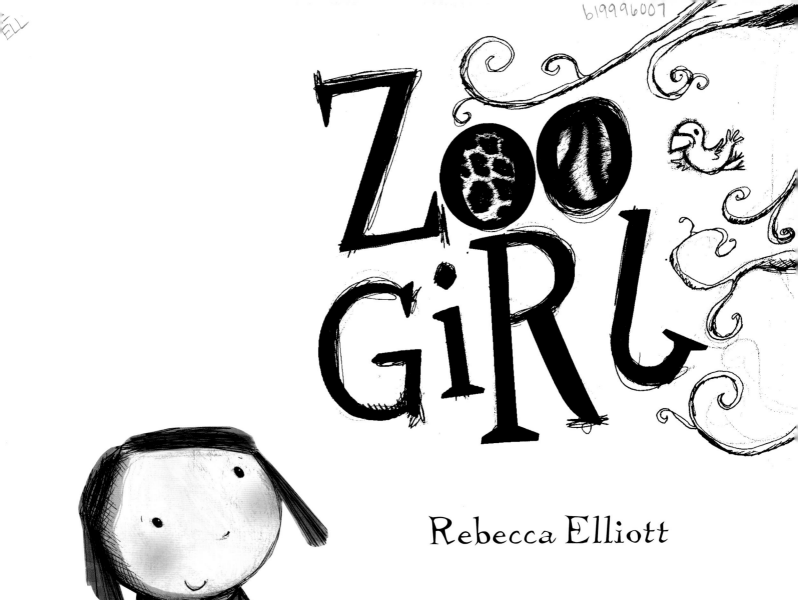

Rebecca Elliott

LION
CHILDREN'S

No family

Alone.

At home!

Left behind

"A child?"

Friends

Living wild!

Discovered

Wanted.

A family.